For Lulu

Text copyright © 2015 by Suzanne Lang
Jacket art and interior illustrations copyright © 2015 by Max Lang
Horse illustration copyright © Rikke Asbjorn
Floral wallpaper pattern copyright © Depositphotos.com/Alexandr Labetskiy

Visit us on the Web! randomhouse.com/kids

Educators and librarians, for a variety of teaching tools, visit us at
RHTeachersLibrarians.com

Library of Congress Cataloging-in-Publication Data
Lang, Suzanne.
Families, families, families! / by Suzanne Lang ; illustrated by Max Lang. — First edition.
pages cm.
Summary: "A host of animals portrays all kinds of non-traditional families." —Provided by publisher.
ISBN 978-0-553-49938-4 (trade) — ISBN 978-0-375-97426-7 (lib. bdg.) — ISBN 978-0-553-49939-1 (ebook)
[1. Stories in rhyme. 2. Families—Fiction. 3. Animals—Fiction.] i. Lang, Max, illustrator. ii. Title.
PZ8.3.L27672Fam 2015 [E]—dc23 2014011623

Book design by John Sazaklis

MANUFACTURED IN CHINA

10 9 8 7 6 5 4 3 2 1

First Edition

Random House Children's Books supports the First Amendment and celebrates the right to read.

FAMILIES, FAMILIES, FAMILIES!

by
**Suzanne Lang
& Max Lang**

Random House New York

Some children have lots of siblings.

Some children have none.

Some children have two dads.

Some have one mom.

Some children live with their grandparents . . .

and some live with an aunt.

Some children have many pets . . .

and some just have a plant!

Some children live with their father.

Some children have two mothers.

Some children are adopted.

Some have stepsisters and—brothers.

Some children bunk with their cousins.

Some have a mom and a pop.

Some children's parents are married.

Some children's parents are not.

So no matter if you have

a ma,

a pa,

a hog,

this llama,

ten frogs and a slug,

a cousin named Doug,

a Great-Grandma Betty
and a Great-Aunt Sue,

Uncles Hal,
Al, and Sal,
and Uncle Lou, too,

one stepsis, three stepbros,
two stepmoms, and a prize-winning rose,

a robot butler
to serve you tea,

the world's biggest grandpa,

or whatever it might be . . .

. . . if you love each other,
then you are a family.